DATE DUE

APR 22		
MAY 06		
SEP 3 0 1992		
FEB. 0 3 1994		
SEP. 0 8 2003		

HIGHSMITH 45-227

A Troll, a Truck, and a Cookie

FOLLETT DOUBLE SCOOP BOOKS

The Troll Family Stories
  Hi, Dog!
  A Dog Is Not a Troll
  Go, Wendall, Go!
  I Love Wheels
  Etta Can Get It!
  A Troll, a Truck, and a Cookie

Other series of Follett Double Scoop Books:
The Cora Cow Tales
The Adventures of Pippin

A Troll, a Truck, and a Cookie

Phylliss Adams
Eleanore Hartson
Mark Taylor

Illustrated by Dennis Hockerman

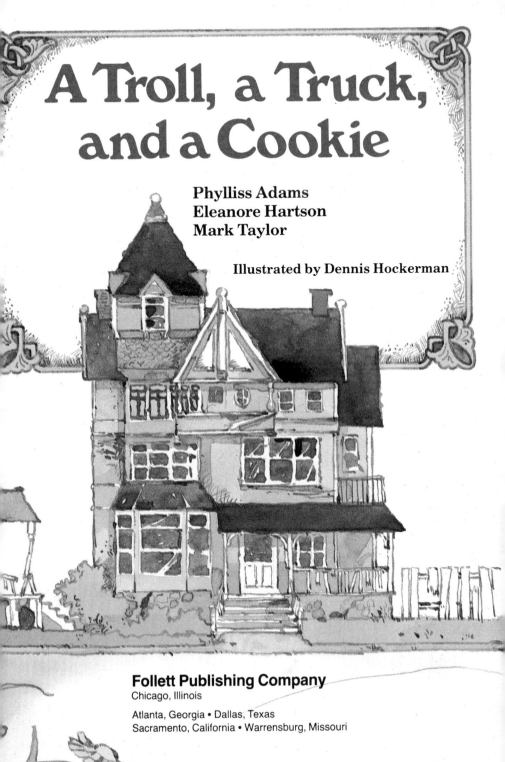

Follett Publishing Company
Chicago, Illinois

Atlanta, Georgia • Dallas, Texas
Sacramento, California • Warrensburg, Missouri

LC 81–17412
ISBN 0–695–41617–0
ISBN 0–695–31617–6 (pbk.)

"Look!" said Leona.

"Look," said Wendall.
"I can not see a house.
I see a green truck.
I see a blue truck.
I can not see a house!"

"I love this house," said Leona.
"I love this little, little house."

"It is the troll house," said Etta.
"It can not come down."

"We want this house," said Blossom.
"We have to have this house.
It is the troll house.
It can not come down."

Not a troll saw the truck.
The big, big truck.

Not a troll saw the wheels.
The big, big wheels.

"Can we jump down?" said Leona.

"We can not jump down," said Etta.

"We have to ride in the house."

"I love this!" said Blossom.

"You love this?" said Wendall.

"I love this ride," said Blossom.

"Have a cookie," said Leona.
"A cookie can help you work."

"We love to help," said Blossom.
"Have a cookie."

15

"This is a ride I love,"
said Wendall.

"Not me," said Etta.
"A house with wheels
is not a house for me."

"This is it," said Wendall.
"The house can go here."

"I love it here," said Buddy.
"And Dandy Dog can run and play."

"We can make money here," said Etta.

"We can?" said Leona.

"We can!" said Etta.

"You see," said Etta.
"We can make money with
the troll cookie."

"It is work," said Leona.

"And it is play," said Wendall.

22

Come to the troll house.
Have a cookie.
A Troll Cookie!

The Troll Word Book

big   See the big dog.

blue   The balloon is blue.

green   This money is green.

little   See the <u>little</u> truck.

run   A dog can <u>run</u>.

saw   Leona <u>saw</u> the red house.

A Troll, a Truck, and Funny Things

Look for things that are wrong in
the picture. Then look in this book on
pages 16 and 17 to check your answers.

Troll House Cookies

To make the cookies, get these things:

someone to help

½ cup peanut butter

Then do these things:

1. Put peanut butter and chips in pan.

2. Heat slowly and stir until melted.

3. Mix in cereal gentl

6 oz. chocolate chips

5 cups crispy cereal

measuring cup, tablespoon, pan, and waxed paper

Drop cookies from spoon onto waxed paper.

5. Chill until set.

hen have a cookie. A Troll Cookie!

A Troll, a Truck, and a Cookie is the sixth book of the Troll Family Stories for beginning readers. All words used in the story are listed here. (The words in darker print were introduced in this book. The other words were introduced in earlier books.)

a	for	Leona	said
and	go	**little**	**saw**
big	**green**	look	see
Blossom		love	the
blue	have		this
Buddy	help	make	to
	here	me	troll
can	**house**	money	**truck**
come	I	not	
cookie	in		want
Dandy Dog	is	play	we
down	it	ride	Wendall
		run	wheels
Etta	jump		with
			work
			you

About the Authors

Phylliss Adams, Eleanore Hartson, and Mark Taylor have a combined background that includes writing books for children and teachers, teaching at the elementary and university levels, and working in the areas of curriculum development, reading instruction and research, teacher training, parent education, and library and media services.

About the Illustrator

Since his graduation from Layton School of Art in Milwaukee, Wisconsin, Dennis Hockerman has concentrated primarily on art for children's books, magazines, greeting cards, and games.

The artist lives and works in his home in Mequon, Wisconsin, with his wife and two children. The children enjoyed many hours in their dad's studio watching as the Troll Family characters came to life.

123456789/868584838